Neighboring

Stories from the Heart of Kentucky

Mark Mattmiller

Neighboring
Copyright © 2013

by Mark Mattmiller

For information, address Cloud 9 Press,
PO Box 385, Lexington, KY 40588.
ISBN: 978-0-9847286-9-5

Cover and illustrations by Chris Epling
Interior design and layout by Chip Holtzhauer

Cloud **Press**

Dedication

Thanks to my wife Linda.

Special thanks to Jack DuArte

Contents

Remnant

E rnie Stone pulled through his barn-lot gate, shut down his old 1951 8N Ford tractor, and stepped off to shut the gate behind him. He heard the familiar whistle of Jake Barnes coming from the direction of Jake's gate thirty yards away. For forty years, they had farmed across the highway from each other, and it had become the practice of each to whistle and wave if they spotted the other during the course of their work. Often, in the last few years, the short whistle and wave evolved into a prolonged visit at the gate, and this day would be no exception. Ernie got back on his tractor, restarted it, and headed across the highway to the wide gravel pull off place where Jake was waiting.

Jake watched as Ernie and his tractor approached. He mused to himself how familiar the picture was. There was Ernie with a "let's get to work" look on his face, the old, almost ancient, little tractor purring, and the work trailer with the perfectly organized tools following both. But, something was different: Ernie was a little slouched, his face a little drawn, and he seemed tense. Jake knew that the news was not necessarily going to be good.

When Ernie pulled off the highway and onto Jake's extended drive, the first words out of his mouth were, "Well, somebody bought it." Ordinarily he would have said, "How's it going?" or something teasing like, "Now what have you messed up?" This time his words were curious. He said just, "Well, somebody bought it."

The "it" Ernie referred to was an old farm known around Mt. Zion as the Wright place. The 250 acre farm had belonged to an absentee owner by the name of Wilson Wright. He lived miles away in Lexington and never visited his land; in fact, hardly anyone in the area even remembered him or his having bought the farm. When he passed away, his daughters put the farm up for sale, and it had remained unsold for over two years.

The Wright farm was huge when compared to the usual farms around Mt. Zion, but what made it most unusual was its stand of old-growth timber. With the exception of a couple of acres of narrow road frontage, the entire farm was covered in woodland. The land had been left untended for over a century, and it had grown back into a magnificent and deep woods. It was a remnant of what it had once been.

The Wright place joined Ernie's farm all along the back of his 60 acres. While that was important to Ernie, the sale of it affected him in a much more profound way. For his entire adult life, Ernie had cut across a small slice of the Wright farm to get to another farm that his son owned. Ernie's son, "Rocky" Stone, was the county sheriff and had little time to farm. He relied on his father to tend to his land. Without the short-cut, it was a four mile drive on the highway. In addition to Ernie's son, two brothers, Shorty and Peachy Cornett, also had farms on the other side of the Wright place. They all shared equipment and labor. Never a day went by that the old logging road through the Wright farm wasn't used by one or all of them in the course of their farming and neighboring. Using the highway to move equipment and tractors would be a significant inconvenience.

At the gate, Jake responded to Ernie's revelation that the place had sold. "Who bought it?" he asked.

"Four guys from somewhere away from here. From out of state, I think." He looked at his feet while he kicked around a little in the gravel before adding, "They said they bought it to hunt on. They will only be here on weekends."

"You talked to them?" asked Jake.

"Yeah, and what's worse, they say they aren't going to allow anyone on the place."

Jake immediately understood the implications to Ernie; and he asked, "Did you tell them you cut through there all the time?"

"Yeah, but they're going to fence it off anyway. They didn't seem to care." Then after a moments silence, he added, "Well, it's theirs, they can do with it what they want, and what they want is nobody on their place."

"If they don't want any trespassers, the best thing they can do is let you keep using the cut-through. They don't know how it works."

What Jake knew was that the best way to keep strangers off your own property was to invite your neighbors onto it. Around Mt. Zion, the practice had worked for generations. Neighbors moved freely from farm to farm. Tools were borrowed, ponds fished, and coons hunted. Permission had been granted years in the past, and it was understood. The land of others was treated with ultimate respect, and the benefit was the extra pair of eyes that would spot and report a downed fence, a sick calf, or anything else that looked out of the way. Jake also knew that if the new owners of the big woods would allow Ernie to continue using the short-cut and asked him to keep everyone else off the land,

Ernie would have treated their request with a reverence. He would have made it a point to patrol the place and advise the occasional visitor to get off.

When Ernie said again, "Well, it is theirs," Jake knew intuitively that Ernie was, in fact, hurt by the banishment. He had used the short cut for years and had always taken care of the place.

* * *

McBride's was a combination small grocery and farm supply store at the northeast crossroads corner in the little community of Mt. Zion, Kentucky. Most every evening and during the day if the weather was bad, there was an ongoing game of Rook or euchre at the table in front by the big window. Sometimes several people could be sitting and waiting their turn to play the winners; they would watch intently as the game progressed. McBride's was the place to be.

The store was the nerve center and heart of community life in and around Mt. Zion and had been for decades. All the comings and goings of local interest were passed along from mouth to mouth at the store. The first question asked by most everybody who entered was something along the lines of, "What's the latest?" There were always a few loafers, or a lone shopper, or Mr. McBride himself to fill in the person asking for news. The status of the crops, the weather forecast, who was sick, and who borrowed what from whom was almost always covered. Certainly, the news of the new owners of the Wright place and Ernie's dilemma had been the hot topic for a few days. Ernie Stone was well liked. He was always the first to give help wherever it was needed. His treatment by the new owners was not seen in a good light. As is always the way, the Mt. Zion folks were forming an opinion of their new neighbors.

Mt. Zion itself was a tight, close-made little place. The community was a remote crossroads hamlet comprised of 10 to12 small houses on the highway that ran through the little settlement. In addition, there was a radiator shop, two churches, the cemetery, McBride's store, and Riggs' service station. Two side streets, each with a handful of houses, completed the picture of Mt. Zion. The area around Mt. Zion was red-clay hill country. The farms were mostly small and poor. There were nice, flat, and productive ridge lands that gave way to draws or hollows on each side. The sloping hillsides were used for pasture and hay fields; usually the steepest were wooded. Sometimes there was a narrow bottom along the creeks and branches at the foot of a hill.

The culture of close-knit neighbors sharing work and equipment was established when the community was first settled. The hilly country and narrow ridges provided just enough cropland for each family to grow an acre or two of burly tobacco, and the warm moist nights offered the perfect conditions for curing the crop. Raising a tobacco crop was an exceptionally labor intensive endeavor. The microscopic seeds were mixed with sand and raked into a covered seed-bed early in the spring, and after the last chance of frost, the plants were pulled by hand from the beds and set into the carefully prepared fields. The soil had been plowed, harrowed more than once, and smoothed over and over with a heavy wooden drag. Before the crops were harvested, the weeds had to be chopped out, suckers broken off, and tobacco worms extracted. Right before cutting time, when the tops were broken off of each plant, the tobacco sticks had to be dropped along the rows.

When the ripe tobacco plants were ready to harvest, the labor requirements multiplied. Day after day, the whole community rotated from farm to farm depending upon the readiness of each crop. Some would be cutting the plants and spearing them onto the tobacco sticks on one farm while others would be loading the wagons on another. A third group of men could very well be housing the crop in the barns on still a different farm at the same time. There was exactness in how the labor was distributed, and there was certainly a precision in how the work progressed. The men invariably worked well together. It was necessary for efficiency and imperative for their survival.

The land was marginally productive, and the farms were small, but for generations, tobacco provided the cash crop that sustained them. Because of the nature of the farms, the land, and the labor, sharing of time and tools cemented the community to itself. But things had changed. The recent demise of the tobacco subsidy program coupled with the trend of taking jobs off the farm, made farm life much less reliant upon a cash crop.

What did not change was the culture of helping others with farm work and the sharing of resources. Today most of the work was done on the weekends and in the evenings after work. Cattle production became the primary farming enterprise. Hay was cut, raked, and baled. Pastures were mowed and fences maintained. Calving time meant checking the herd twice a day. Cold weather meant feeding every day. And twice a year, the cows were put up, sorted, and worked by the veterinarian. In some ways, because of the hours at work off the farm, the old tradition of neighbor helping neighbor was just as important as it had ever been.

* * *

Peachy Cornett was a big man. He was unusually loud and boisterous, but almost always in a pleasant and teasing way. Peachy was not teasing when he hit the door at McBride's store. He was red-faced and obviously perturbed when he addressed the small gathering of card players. "Three signs! Did you all see it? Those bastards put up three no trespassing signs at the gate. There's one on the gate and one nailed to trees on each side."

"Yeah, I saw," replied one card player.

"What signs, what gate?" asked Harold Browning. Harold was the oldest man in the community, and he was almost always at the store.

"That broken down gate at the Wright place. They put up three friggen signs!"

"You've got to be kidding!" Harold half shouted.

"And after that bull-shit with Ernie," someone added.

"They must think we're blind," said Peachy as his

face reddened a little more and his voice rose."

"Ain't that a crock of shit?"

"Ernie says there's signs all around the whole farm."

"Two of them came into the store Tuesday. They didn't have much to say," added McBride.

"Real friendly bunch, huh?" asked Harold sarcastically.

"Well they sure don't act like they care much for us," bellowed Peachy Cornett.

"To hell with them," Harold said. "It belongs to them now, and they can do with it whatever they want."

"Yeah, but it don't mean we have to like it."

* * *

Jake Barnes knew that the new owners of the old woods showed up nearly every weekend. He had put all his jobs on hold for the coming Saturday morning and was determined to find the men and make one last appeal on Ernie's behalf. He had heard that Harold Browning and Mr. McBride had both lobbied for Ernie and his short-cut and had gotten absolutely nowhere, but he was determined to try it himself. He called Shorty Cornett late Friday to find out if he had seen any sign of them. Shorty said that he hadn't seen anything, but there had been a lot of racket: he had heard what he thought were chain saws and four wheelers. That was enough for Jake.

When Saturday morning came, Jake walked down the highway the short distance to the gate at the Wright place, climbed over it, and started the descent that would take him into the big woods. The ten-acre field along the highway was the last on the big farm to have been tended. Ernie Stone and Peachy Cornett had square-baled it seven or eight years earlier. The terrain sloped off to the left and towards the headwaters of Rock Creek.

Small cedar trees were abundant on the little piece, and except for a few redbuds, the cedars were the only trees visible. As he started through the abandoned field, Jake saw where someone had cut one of the cedars at ground level. He surmised that it had been cut for a Christmas tree. Since no cattle had been in to the field to nip the tops off the trees when they were small, they had grown straight and true with only one stalk and a nice shape. The brush, weeds, and briars between the trees made walking difficult, but Jake stayed on what was left of the old rock road along the lower side where the going was easy. Jake was surprised by the evidence of recent A.T.V. traffic.

He reached the lower end of the field and sat for a moment on what had been the front steps of an ancient log house. A few stones around the former foundation and the standing stone chimney were all that remained. The old home-site was a mere suggestion of what it must have been in the days of its usefulness, but it remained just as Jake remembered it when he first saw it as a young boy. As he sat, Jake found himself reminiscing about earlier walks he had made through the field, along the creek, and into the big woods. His memory of his first visit to the farm was clouded, but Jake believed he had accompanied his father on a search for a missing calf, cow, coon hound, or something. He was quite sure of his last trip: he had taken his sister's kid for a walk into the woods looking for buckeyes and mistletoe.

When Jake left the old home-site, he followed the road as it dipped down and away from the cedar field, crossed the trickling creek, and entered a forest of much larger trees. The old farm had been abandoned in three different stages: first, the huge old-growth timber at the back of the place, then the center of the farm where Jake entered, and lastly, the small cedar and weed field by the highway. From where the path crossed the creek, Jake walked up and off to his left looking for any sign of the new owners.

Scattered sparsely were the huge sprawling seed-oaks that were there when the pasture was abandoned. They were ancient. Some were dead, and some were dying. Surrounding them were the tall straight white oak, hickory, and ash trees that were in prime health and growing. These straight trees had competed for sunlight and grown forty or so feet straight up to where they formed a gentle canopy that mostly shaded the forest floor. Enough sunlight filtered through to provide an occasional splotch on the leaf covered ground. The cedars that once covered these fields couldn't survive the competition for sunlight, and only a few survived. They were mostly fully grown, but slowly dying for lack of sun. Random and rotting cedar skeletons could be seen lying about. The walking here was not as mean as in the small field by the road. Only an occasional multifloral rose, a few maverick weeds, and some scattered sprouts from the windblown seeds of the ash and maple trees grew from the forest floor. The ground was a thick mat of dead leaves, hickory casings, decaying acorns, small limbs, and sticks.

Jake angled back down the wooded hillside to follow the creek that would take him to the deepest part of the forest. He stopped abruptly when he spotted a new elaborate tree-stand built high in the branches of a big red oak. When he approached the stand, he noticed that five or six alleyways had been cut out of the woods and away from the deer stand like bicycle spokes. These narrow clearings began at the stand and continued for about fifty yards each. Their function was obvious. The clear paths would make it easy for a hunter sitting in the stand to shoot and kill any deer that crossed them. When Jake approached the stand, he also saw the ruts and trails that four wheelers had cut into the deep humus of the forest floor. He paused for a few seconds, looked down and around, and remembered Ernie's words, "Well it's theirs, and they can do with it whatever they want."

He left the deer stand and walked back down to the old road that paralleled the creek. The road was mostly cleared and beat down by the A.T.V. traffic. At the very edge of the oldest and largest part of the farm, there was a cold-water spring above the creek. The spring was nestled between two giant sycamore trees and years ago somebody had rocked in a small basin that became a reservoir for the cool water. An old enameled blue and white speckled dipper hung from one of the trees. Jake took down the dipper, rinsed it in the water flowing out of the basin, and drank deeply from the spring. He knew the dipper had been there for years, and he began to reminisce again. He wondered just how many times he had stopped and used the dipper to drink. He wondered how many others had drunk from the old dipper. Who did the dipper actually belong to?

Jake entered the ancient woods. Here the trees were majestic. They were two to three feet in diameter and grew seventy-five to a hundred feet straight up. Each had just one trunk, with no side branches, until almost the very top where the branches reached out and formed a dense canopy. Little sunlight penetrated, and the forest was in a permanent semi-darkness. Cedar trees were long gone, and only the hardwoods remained. The forest floor was thick with humus and clear of all weeds and undergrowth; walking here was as easy as walking on a sidewalk. The air was void of dust and pollen and within it hung a sweetness and a tranquility. There was also a myriad of subtle sounds in the great woods. There were the cries and singing of countless birds, the rattle of a squirrel gnawing on an acorn or hickory, the slightest murmur of a multitude of insects, the crash of a drop of dew as it hits the leaves after falling from the top of one of the giant trees, and always the far away cry of that vigilant crow. The forest was alive with a perpetual serenity.

The serenity was shattered by the unmistakable sound of approaching four-wheelers. Jake stood absolutely still as that intrusive sound came closer and closer. He was standing within ten feet of one of the trails worn down into the forest floor, and he anticipated that they would pass right by him. He was looking up the hill and through the giant trees towards the sounds when he got his first glimpse of the four-wheelers. He counted three of them as they flashed through the open spaces between the trees. Jake realized he had guessed right as they started down the hill and directly towards him. The first and the second passed within ten feet of Jake and didn't see him, but the third pulled up next to him and stopped.

The man on the four-wheeler was middle aged and was mostly bald. He wore a camouflaged jacket and jeans. One of the men who had passed Jake turned around and came back. He also wore the camouflaged jacket and jeans, but he was not as old as the first and had a mop of blonde curly hair. They both remained seating on their A.T.V.. The older man asked in a direct voice, "What do you want? What are you doing here?"

Jake responded, "I am Jake Barnes. I live right across the highway, and I came in here to see you, to talk to you."

"About what?" asked the curly headed one.

"I wanted to ask you, to plead with you, to allow our neighbor, Ernie Stone, to continue to cut through your farm. He's a good guy. He will take care of your land. It would make a big difference to him, and really, to all of us." said Jake.

The older man was polite but frank when he replied, "I'm sorry Mr. Barnes, but we've already discussed it, and we've made up our minds. We aren't allowing anyone on the property."

Jake recognized the finality of their decision and said, "Well, good to meet you, I'll just be going on." He turned to walk away.

"Bye, now," said the curly one sardonically.

"Sorry, sir," said the older, bald man.

Jake started back the way he came in. He was contemplative and a bit discouraged by his failure. He thought the whole thing was unfair. It was unfair to Ernie, and, in essence, to everyone. As he walked, he began to wonder who had settled the old farm, and he found himself thinking about some of the old-timers who had lived and farmed around there long ago. When he got to the spring, he picked up the dipper and drank again. Jake thought about just taking the dipper with him: take it to his own farm. He stood there for a minute or two with the dipper in his hand, and then he hung it back on the tree and turned to walk home.

* * *

It was in the early evening of the following Saturday when one of the new owners showed up again at the store. It was the curly headed one. He looked tense and unhappy when he came through the screen door. In fact, he was a little forceful when he addressed the group of card players, "Would any of you guys happen to know who tore down the signs at my gate?"

"Signs?" someone asked.

"Yeah, we had three signs posted at the gate, and someone tore down two of them. Threw them on the ground."

No one in the group said a word, but they did look at each other with that old familiar look of bewilderment: eyes widened, shoulders shrugged, and palms lifted up.

"Well," the new owner said, "I sure would like to find out who did it!"

It was just then that Peachy Cornett started to

raise himself out of his chair. He slowly unfolded his huge frame, stood still for a second, and then moved towards the newcomer. An absolute hush fell over the room. When they were face to face, Peachy looked down at the man and in a voice that was hardly more than a whisper said, "Listen Curly, quit your bellyaching. Around here, one sign has always been enough."

With that, he pulled down the bill of his cap, turned around, and walked out.

The Complement

Old Jake Barnes made the five mile trip from his home in the tiny town of Mt. Zion, Kentucky to his red-clay hill farm almost every day. Except for three calves, he no longer raised cattle or crops. Jake retired from the post office several years earlier, and at this time, his farming activities were mostly limited to keeping the hillsides mowed, the fences mended, and the barn in good repair. He worked slowly now and rarely more than a couple of hours a day.

On this crisp December Saturday, Jake was at the old farm waiting for his son, Henry. The two men, a middle aged son and his father, were to finish up the annual job of getting in the firewood that they would both burn in their fireplaces. Once or twice a month, Henry made the forty-five minute trip from his home in the city to help out around the place. However, this fall he visited the farm and his father more often while they worked with the firewood. Cutting, splitting, and loading the wood was mean and tough labor, and Jake needed his son's help.

Jake knew that his son wouldn't arrive for at least another hour, but still, he caught himself occasionally watching for Henry to come driving down the gravel driveway. He had a couple of small jobs that he wanted to finish before Henry arrived, and as was always his way, he wasted no time in getting started. He hooked a log chain to the drawbar of his small tractor, wrapped it around the lift arms, and backed out of the barn. Earlier in the week, he had discovered that a metal gate he had left leaning against an old water tank had fallen down. The fescue grass and weeds had grown around, over, and through the pipes and wires of the gate, and when Jake tried to lift the gate, he was unable to budge it; the gate was bound too tightly by the grass.

After backing the tractor up to the gate, but before hooking the chain to it, Jake tried once more to lift it up; again he found that it was just too much for him. In his prime, Jake was known for his strength, and as he stood and looked at the gate, he wondered if it would have presented such a challenge to him in earlier days. He frowned first and then smiled to himself as he reminisced.

The chain drew taut, and as the tractor eased away, the gate rose up and out of the grass. Jake got down off the tractor to unhook the chain, and he saw immediately that the strain had been too much for the old gate; it was bent and broken beyond repair. He climbed back onto the tractor to drag the gate across the hay field and down to the old sinkhole where outdated implements, old

fence, and other junk had been dumped since the place was first settled.

As he started across the field, Jake observed how the cloud cover had increased as the morning passed. A cold wind was steady and coming directly out of the northwest. Jake pulled his coat tighter around his neck and hunkered down a little as he drove the tractor. Again he looked towards the sky, and he absorbed the biting breeze. Jake's observations told him that it would snow for certain before nightfall.

While he was unloading the gate at the dumpsite, Jake noticed that several large pieces had broken off as it was dragged through the field. He knew it would be easy to find the debris as he followed the tire tracks back up through the hayfield. Jake climbed up onto the tractor, restarted it, and headed back to the barn.

On the return trip, Jake had to get down off the tractor twice and pick up parts of the broken gate. He began to count to himself how many times that day he had climbed off and back onto his tractor. For Jake, it wasn't as easy as it once was. A little arthritis and a lot of age were challenging Jake's stoicism.

As he neared the barn, Jake saw that his son, Henry, had arrived and was busy at the small work trailer. Jake knew that Henry would be sharpening the chainsaws and making sure they had gasoline and oil. He approached the trailer, turned the tractor around, backed up, and shut it off. Henry hitched the trailer to the drawbar.

"Hello, Son, I'm glad you're here," Jake smiled and spoke while getting down from the tractor.

"Yeah, Pop, me too," Henry answered as they shook hands. "Cold isn't it?"

"It is for sure. It's going to snow."

"You think so?" asked Henry. "The weatherman didn't say anything about snow."

"Look at the sky, Son. It's been filling in all morning," Jake said, "and the temperature's been dropping. It's going to snow."

They shared a little small talk as they double-checked to make sure they had loaded up everything they would need. Then Henry climbed up on the tractor to drive, and Jake sat on the tailgate of the work trailer. They started down the steep hillside and headed into the woods to work. Henry knew exactly where they were going and where they would start.

There was an old red oak that had fallen several years before, and the men had spotted it the last time out. They had decided then that they would work on it next. Old, long-dead red-oaks were their first choice of wood for the fireplace. Henry left the frozen grass-covered access road that paralleled the small creek running through the woods. He turned onto an old logging road and followed it up the rise and deep into the woodland. The road provided the only access into the upper woods, and it was rarely used except by the deer, wild turkeys, and other wildlife.

The ancient field that the men passed through had been abandoned for agricultural use a century earlier. Scattered throughout the hillside were the huge sprawling seed-oaks that were there when the field was abandoned. They were the oldest trees still living on the old pasture. Some were dead, and some were dying. Surrounding them were the tall straight white oak, hickory, and ash trees that were in prime health and growing. These tall trees had competed for sunlight and grown forty or so feet straight up to where, during the summer months, they formed a gentle canopy that mostly shaded the forest floor. The cedars that once covered these fields couldn't survive the competition for sunlight, and only a few survived. They were mostly fully grown but slowly dying for lack of sun. The air was always sweet, fresh, and dust-free. Even during the winter months, and on a bleak and dreary day, the quiet woods evoked a sense of tranquility and serenity.

The tractor broke the hush of the woods as father and son approached the red oak and the point where the hillside was becoming too steep for the tractor. Henry shut down the engine and climbed off the tractor as Jake slid off the trailer tailgate. The two men unloaded their tools and went right to work.

As Jake and Henry toiled, it was obvious that the two men had spent a lot of time working together. They rarely spoke, and their labor presented a clear picture of coordination. The movements of one man always seemed to complement the work of the other: the splitting wedge was handed over at just the right moment; the limb held and pulled for the chainsaw without even a nod; the cut logs set up on end for splitting, all without wasted time or effort.

Operating the chainsaws was always dangerous and strenuous work, and except on very rare occasions, Henry did all of the sawing. His father was just not steady enough to be handling them much, and he tired easily when he did. It had only been in the last two or three years that Henry had assumed this role. Always before, Jake had been the one to do the heavy work, but now it was understood that those days were behind him. His role had changed from the leader and teacher to the helper and observer, and Jake watched his son with satisfaction.

The men worked on cutting and splitting the old red-oak for about an hour, and they had both heated up so much that they had shucked their hooded Carhartts and were working in their bibbed overalls and flannel shirts. The split wood was stacked high on the trailer, and there was enough left piled up on the ground to make another full load. The saws, axes, and wedges were placed on top of the stacked wood, and the men put their coats back on for the return trip to the barn. There wasn't room on the trailer for a passenger, so Henry stood on the tractor drawbar while Jake drove.

Rather than try to turn the tractor and trailer around on the narrow pathway, Jake continued the way they were headed. The old road dropped off shortly and headed straight down to the creek road. When they had gone about half way down the steep hill, they were forced to stop. There was an impassable barricade created by the damage from a severe ice-storm the winter before.

"Looks like more work, Pop."

"Yeah, but we've got no choice," Jake responded. "Let's see what we've got here."

The men got off the tractor and approached a jumbled mess of limbs and vines. Two branches of a mid-sized locust tree had been broken down by the weight of the ice. They had not separated entirely from the trunk of the tree but were still attached by bark and some wood fragments. Both limbs had dropped on a third stout limb of an adjacent hickory, and all three were suspended across the trail a little higher than eye level. The hickory limb, about five inches in diameter, had not broken but was only bent by the weight of the other two. A large grapevine dropping from the tree tops to the end of the hickory limb helped to support the parallel and twisted branches. The three limbs were impossibly bound by gravity and entanglement.

Henry and Jake stood and looked at the obstruction, and after a few seconds, Henry said, "Hand

me the small saw, Pop."

Jake walked to the back of the trailer and picked up the smaller of the two chainsaws. When he handed it to Henry, he warned, "Be careful."

What the two men both realized as they studied the tangled branches was that two of the most elementary rules of the woodsman had to be broken in order to cut through the clutter. First, the chain saw would have to be held up higher than the cutter's head; secondly, two limbs together should never be cut with a power saw. They were getting into a situation that both men recognized was potentially dangerous.

Henry started the saw and slowly walked around and under the entanglement. As the saw idled, he walked back to where he started. He stood and calculated for about half a minute. Henry was trying to decide what would be the best and safest way to approach the cutting. He walked around to the other side again and stood there studying the limbs for another few moments. Jake was eyeing the problem as well, but the noise from the saw made communications difficult. Finally, in an unexpected move, Henry exhaled, turned to face Jake, and handed the running saw to his father.

Old Jake nodded and took the saw. Without hesitation, he made two deep cuts on the bottom of the 5 inch hickory limb. Next, he made deeper cuts on the top side of both locust branches. When he then walked to the grapevine and cut through it, all three limbs snapped, sagged, dropped, and separated. When the limbs separated, the tricky part was over. Jake handed the saw back to his son, and it was a routine and simple job for him to cut the limbs into smaller pieces while Jake dragged them out of the way.

"Well, that's that," Henry said when they had finished, and they started back down the hill, Jake driving and Henry back standing on the drawbar. They went straight to the creek road without any additional delays.

About halfway through the woods, the old road crossed over a small wet-weather rivulet. The crossing had been built up over the years with field stones and rocks from the woods. When the tractor approached the fill, Henry tapped his father on the shoulder and gave him the signal to shut off the tractor. He needed to free up his hands to zip his hooded Carhartt jacket. The cold wind was picking up and getting to both men. While zipping and re-arranging his jacket, Henry noticed that the crossing was sinking and more rocks were needed.

"Looks like we need a little more rock in here, Pop."

"Yeah, maybe I can get to it when we finish with the firewood," Jake answered. "It's been awhile since we added any."

"Let's catch a warm day. I'll help."

When they left the old road and headed up the hill, the first few flakes of snow began to fall. Henry smiled to himself, but Old Jake barely noticed. He was in deep thought and planning when and where to get the rock for the crossover.

Schooled

Jimmy Filson was a senior at Hawkinsville High School. He was a big, strong farm boy who lived with his parents on the edge of town. After school, he could almost always be found at home helping his father on their tobacco and cattle farm. During school, he was polite and punctual. Everybody thought of Jimmy as a good kid. Neither athletics nor academics were necessarily his strengths. His interests lay in the areas of farming and mechanics, and he applied himself earnestly to the study of both.

After the school lunch each day, Jimmy and two friends headed to the gym to shoot a few baskets and relax before the time came to go back to class. They had been doing this since they were freshmen, and this day in November was no different. The boys had just begun to shoot around when Amos Ray, the principal, walked in and approached them. He was a little red in the face and was obviously angry.

He walked up to the boys, raised his chin up high, and half shouted, "I've told you before, there are no more breaks! If you've got time to mess around in here, you've got time to get up there and get your minds on taking those tests!"

One of the young men said, "Yes sir," and they all three turned around to put the basketballs up and leave the gym. They reacted to the admonishment with a slow gait and slumped shoulders, but just before exiting through the side door, Jimmy turned and gave the principal a little smile. Anyone who happened to see that and who knew Jimmy well would say he probably had a little trick up his sleeve.

The "tests" Principal Ray referred to were the upcoming ACT College Entrance Exams that were implemented to replace the old State Core Content Tests. Every student in the state was now required to take the ACT. Several years earlier, in an effort to get the state's overall educational level off the bottom, the state General Assembly passed the Educational Reform Act. The Legislators poured significant money into its implementation, and that led, of course, to the necessity for some method of accountability and assessment. The annual student accountability exams to verify improvement were the result. Later, the introduction of the No Child Left Behind initiative created a movement towards nationalizing the curriculums, and one by one, states were adopting the ACT to test all students. Hawkinsville students would now be measured

against students from across the country.

The school and the Hawkinsville/Mt.Zion Independent School District as a whole had been under intense pressure to improve their scores on the state exams. For the last five years, the test results at Hawkinsville High had remained stagnant and had even decreased in some areas. If the trend did not change, the high school could be deemed a "school in crisis" and face being completely managed by the State Department of Education. State personnel would move in, and the current administration would move aside. In addition, the entire district faced the possibility of a reduction in state funding. The school board and all school employees were feeling the pressure.

Hawkinsville was a small town in a rural farming community, and the school district included the residents of the much smaller Mt.Zion, Kentucky. The two small towns were only four miles apart, and the highway between them was moderately populated as well. The ten thousand residents of both communities had always taken pride in their tiny independent school system; however, they were becoming increasingly more and more alarmed as the test scores were demonstrating that their school's academic standing was falling behind when compared to the rest of the state. A few parents had even transferred their children to the consolidated county high school. In an effort to halt the tailspin, the Hawkinsville School Board hired Amos Ray as principal of their high school. He was given the job because he convinced the board that his military background, coupled with his experience as an educator in a tough inner city school, gave him the tools to instill the order needed to correct the academic shortfall. He sold himself as being quite the disciplinarian.

During Mr. Ray's two year tenure as principal, he did, in fact, initiate a multitude of changes. His changes were similar in one respect: they all meant more minutes of instruction and less time doing anything else. There was no down time for the students or the teachers. Amos Ray expected every teacher to be engaged in academic instruction from bell to bell. All breaks were cancelled, the times between classes were reduced, lunch periods were shortened, and homerooms were eliminated.

There were those who argued that Ray's methods were counterproductive to the goal of increasing test scores. Many teachers and administrators believed that students would become disenchanted, lose interest, and quit trying. They thought teachers would teach the test, the instruction would become boring, and classroom stagnation would follow. When colleagues questioned the direction of his policies, the principal became demeaning and confrontational. He was developing a reputation as a man who absolutely had to get his way. Amos Ray was shackled to his own agenda. He would listen to no one.

* * *

"What in the hell are you talking about?" School Superintendent, Jerry Brown, asked forcibly. Amos Ray and Jerry Brown were meeting in the board office, and Principal Ray had just revealed a threat made by high school students to sabotage the upcoming tests.

"It's exactly what I just told you, Sir. Those three boys came into my office and asked about getting back the 10 minute break after lunch. Of course I told them that we wouldn't do that. Then that Filson boy smiled and asked what would happen if ninety percent of the students did as poorly as they could on the exams." Amos Ray was breathing heavily.

"Well, hell, that's no problem; just talk them out of it," superintendent Brown replied somewhat loudly.

Ray responded, "I don't know. I don't think I can. They seemed determined. Something in their tone and demeanor made me think they're serious. I believe those boys have talked with the rest of the student body, and they've got plans in the works."

"Well then, just give them back their break. That'll take care of it," Jerry Brown countered.

Amos Ray seemed indignant when he came back with, "No way! I'm not doing that. I've come too far with this thing to start caving in to this kind of bull-shit. Those students are beginning to act like this whole place is all about them."

Jerry Brown's first response was a jaw-dropping, head lifting, lost-in-the-meaning-of-it, blank stare. After a moment's silence he replied to the principal with, "Now hold on Amos. Let's think here a minute. This could get us in a real mess, a real can of worms."

The principal was uncompromising. He wouldn't relinquish control. "You're not kidding, what if these students start thinking they can always jerk us around like this?"

"I'm more worried about what will happen if they end up throwing the tests than I am who's in charge," Brown said. He was getting a little red in the face.

"So, are you saying you think it will turn out O.K. if the students get their way with this?" Ray asked somewhat defiantly.

"Look, Amos," the superintendent spoke slowly now, "we've been over this time and again. Really, since you first got here. There are those who believe your ways have been too severe, but I've always supported you. I've told you myself, students should have a sense of ownership in their school. They must be made to feel like it is theirs. We all know students have to be in a good frame of mind to take the tests and do well…"

Amos Ray cut the superintendent off with, "And you know I believe that in order to get the scores up, teachers must be teaching every minute, and students must be in there learning!"

"So," said the superintendent, "this is the defining distinction, and it really doesn't help that we see that. We've got a problem here, and it's up to you to fix it. I'm suggesting to you, in the strongest terms, to relax with the kids and give them back their break."

"And I'm telling you, Sir, that I just can't do that," answered Amos Ray.

Jerry Brown turned in his chair and stared out the window for a few seconds. He seemed relaxed when he turned back, looked directly into the principal's eyes, and said, "It's your school Amos, and you'd better get it fixed."

* * *

When Amos Ray went back to the high school and entered his office, he knew his circumstances were desperate. Ray felt a sense of urgency. If even a few students did as poorly as they could on the tests, it would destroy the overall scores for the entire school. If a majority sabotaged the exams, it would be so bad that Hawkinsville High School would become the laughingstock of the entire state. He would surely be fired. On the other hand, if he caved in and gave the break back, he would lose control. He would become the laughingstock.

Principal Ray knew that part of the problem lay in the fact that the students faced no real consequences if they performed poorly on the exams. Only the school and the district would suffer. That was the flaw in the entire system, and schoolteachers everywhere worked overtime to motivate their students to put forth the ultimate effort on testing day. The burden was not on the students, and that was the problem that Amos Ray realized he had to fix.

Later that day the principal smiled to himself as he rethought the plan he had formulated. He was sure of himself: no underage bumpkins could strong-arm Amos Ray. It would take just a few minutes of research and a little organizing, and then he could address the faculty and the student body.

Early the next morning Principal Ray contacted State University to learn what ACT scores were required for admission into the school. These minimum scores were referred to as "benchmarks" and varied for the four content areas of Math, English, Reading, and Science. It was getting tougher and tougher to gain admittance into the university, and the benchmark scores had been systematically increased over the past few years.

As soon as Ray had the benchmark scores, he told his secretary to call all students and faculty to the auditorium. He leaned back in his office chair, closed his eyes, and smiled as he thought of the students' reaction to his plan. The gig is up; the show is over, he thought. Now, they could no longer be unconcerned or complacent about taking the tests.

Amos Ray gave the students plenty of time to get to the auditorium and settle down before he made his way through the school. He walked into the big room, down the aisle, and onto the stage. The students quieted down, and he began to speak, "I have tried to instill in you a sense of pride concerning your education, but you have not responded. Many of you have just not taken your preparation for the upcoming tests seriously, and some of you have suggested that you don't even try. So, I've added a few changes to our testing policy to insure that you make the necessary effort."

At this moment, the secretary and two teachers began to distribute a handout. The principal continued with, "What you are now getting is a list showing the four scores that you must attain when you take the tests this spring. You will have to meet or exceed these benchmarks, or you will not be allowed to graduate. This policy is in keeping with the national trends, and it will not be changed. It is final. Now it's time to go back to class and get serious." The scores reflected exactly what was required for admission to State University.

As the students and teachers looked over the standards, a low murmur began to fill the auditorium. A few moans were heard and then silence. It was unusually quiet as the students filed up the aisles and out of the room.

* * *

Many of the tobacco barns around Hawkinsville and Mt. Zion still had the leaf hanging from the rails. The process of stripping the cured leaves from the stalks had begun. The barns had an attached "stripping" room where the monotonous and time consuming process took place. It was here that the local news was passed along during the slow work. The farmer, his neighbors, children, and possibly his wife would stand at the benches and pass the days pulling the leaf and baling it according to color and condition. A wood stove and a crock-pot with soup or chili were standard features. A radio provided the background to the ongoing conversations, and no topic was off limits. The weather, crops, illnesses, and the high-school ball teams were always hot topics.

On this November afternoon, Jimmy Filson hurried home from school to help his father, Dave; their neighbor, Harold Browning; and Jimmy's uncle, Shorty Cornett, in the stripping room. Shorty was the big brother of "Peachy" Cornett, and unlike his brother he was a short, stout, barrel-chested man. He was known for his strength and his penchant for wearing blue bibbed overalls. He came by his name because he had a "short fuse" and lost his temper quickly, not because of his stature. Harold was an older man and a neighbor who helped the Filsons with their farm work from time to time. Young Jimmy Filson entered the room, offered his greetings, asked where they wanted him, and went straight to work.

After a few minutes, his father said, "You're awfully quiet Jimmy. How was school today?"

"It was all right Dad," the youngster replied.

It may not have been obvious to the others in the stripping room that Jimmy Filson was somehow upset, but his father knew intuitively that something was bothering his son. "All right son," he said after a few more minutes passed, "let's hear it, what's going on?"

"Well, Dad, Mr. Ray called everyone into the auditorium today, and he told us we had to have certain grades on the tests or else we wouldn't graduate," he answered.

"You mean the end of the year tests they've been doing over there?" asked Shorty Cornett.

"Yeah, Uncle Shorty," he said. "Now it's the ACT, and the scores we need are the same as we'd need to get into State University. At least, that's how I think it is."

"That doesn't seem hardly fair to wait until you're seniors to drop this on you. What about you guys who aren't going to college?" Dave Filson asked.

"We wondered that, Dad. A lot of us don't think we can do it, pass it I mean," Jimmy lamented.

"Surely you're mistaken Jimmy. I'm going to walk to the house and call Amos," said Jimmy's father. He was getting tense. And as was always his way, he was determined to act now, not later.

Dave Filson left the stripping room, and the other men went back to work. There were one or two comments about how much things had changed, and then the men worked mostly in silence.

When about ten minutes had passed, Dave Filson entered the stripping room. His face was drawn, and he was not smiling. He waited only a few seconds before he started in: "It didn't go well. We had words. I asked him about it, and he said that Jimmy was right. They have to get certain scores, or they can't graduate. I reminded him that

Jimmy wasn't going to college. He said he had to treat all students the same, so that didn't matter. A lot more was said, and a lot of it was said by me. It didn't end well. He is unyielding."

Jimmy's voice was low and almost breaking when he said, "Dad, I'll try. I hope I can do it. I've not even been close in the pre-tests. But, I'll try."

"Okay Son, okay. Something will work out," Dave Filson said.

It was quiet in the room for a minute or two before Shorty piped in, "That sounds just like something some dumb-ass teacher would dream up. They ought to all have to take it themselves. Hell's bells. If Jimmy can't pass it, I'd bet a dollar to a doughnut about half of the teachers over there can't pass it either."

It was then that Dave Filson's hands stopped the tobacco stripping for just a few seconds. He stood still, turned away from the bench just a little, and looked off for a moment. Then his shoulders dropped, and he got the slightest smile. Shorty's rant about teachers taking the tests had given Dave an idea: an idea he could expand into a strategy. He turned back around and went back to the work. He was mostly quiet the rest of the day.

* * *

Jerry Brown was sure that the situation he was facing was, by far, worse than any he had experienced in his 16 years as school superintendent. The night before, he had met with David Filson and three other men who were all parents of Hawkinsville High students. They were organized, articulate, and especially succinct in voicing their concerns and demands. The meeting lasted for almost two hours, and when it was over, Mr. Brown knew, without a doubt, that he had his hands full.

That morning Superintendent Brown was waiting in his office when two school board members, Everett Juett and Becca Switzer, entered together. They were meeting so that Mr. Brown could explain the details of what had transpired the night before.

As Superintendent Brown explained it, the essence of the parents' presentation was simple. Since no amount of persuasion could get the principal to change his mind about tying graduation to the test scores, it seemed reasonable to them that the teachers should be required to take the same test.

That way they, the parents, could be assured that the problem of low scores was because of the students' indifference and not the result of inadequate instruction or unprepared teachers. If the teachers didn't take the tests, David Filson said that he and at least twenty other families would remove their children from the Hawkinsville Schools and enroll them in county schools. He had apparently already received the go-ahead from the county superintendent. Brown's summary was crisp and to the point when he said, "Our principal, Amos, is getting us into a real mess. If even just a few families transfer to the county, we might as well close up shop."

"I don't believe this!" Everett Juett replied, "The whole town is pissed off. I know my phone has been ringing off the hook. Even the newspaper called."

"Teachers are threatening to unionize!"

"Parents are going to sue!"

"Students say they're going to skip until this is changed."

"Yeah," said Becca Switzer, "where is this thing going?"

"I know where it's not going," said Jerry Brown.

"It's not going any further." He picked up his desk phone and instructed his secretary to get Amos Ray there ASAP.

"This guy is a loose cannon," said Juett. "You've put up with his stuff entirely too long, Jerry."

"I know, I know; he's never listened to a thing I said. I told him time and again to lighten up," Jerry said.

"He's got to go, Jerry," said Everett Juett.

"Yeah, Jerry, he's got to go. He's been pushing and pushing, and now he's gone too far," Becca Switzer agreed.

Before Superintendent Brown could respond, the principal knocked and entered. After shaking hands all around, he sat down, and Jerry Brown began with, "Amos, this thing has gone way past not good. I'm sure you are aware of the uproar, and the explosion about teachers taking the tests."

"Yes, sir, I'm very aware."

"Do you know of the parents' threat to go to the county?" Brown asked.

"Yes, I heard."

"Of course, I'm sure you do realize teachers will

not be taking any tests," continued Jerry Brown.

"Well, they could, you know. Every teacher has a planning period, and they could use that time to...."

The superintendent interrupted Amos Ray. "You don't get it Amos. You just don't get it. There will be no teachers taking tests!"

"Look!" Amos bellowed, "I'm not stopping now. We're too close. No way am I caving in. We can't quit now. We just can't quit!"

Jerry Brown reacted poorly to Ray's use of the word we. He raised the palms of both hands to signal for silence, and after a few seconds, he addressed Amos Ray in a calm but firm voice. "Amos," he said, "I'm not sure how this got to be 'we', but please let this sink in. We have called an emergency meeting of the board for tonight, and we will be deciding what to do about you."

Ray let out a sort of snort, but before he could reply, the superintendent and then the two board members stood up. For Amos Ray the meeting was over. He nodded and left the room, but he was fuming.

* * *

The real excitement for the tiny town of Hawkinsville started the next evening at the high school gym; the local boys were playing their first home basketball game. It is not exactly clear how all of the events unfolded, but the important features were indisputable.

It seems that several men were standing outside the gym entrance smoking and talking when Amos Ray left the gym to get a breath of fresh air. He didn't join the small group of men but stood off by himself. At that time, David Filson, Shorty Cornett, and two other men approached to go into the gym. Principal Amos Ray stopped David Filson and abruptly started in on him. "I'd like to know just one thing. What makes you think you're an expert on education?"

Before Dave could reply, Ray followed with, "Don't you know trouble-makers like you are messing up a lot of hard work?"

"Well...Sir... I...," Dave tried to speak but was immediately interrupted by Amos Ray.

The principal was red-faced and shouting by now. "You all act like you'd rather stay in the dark ages. You want to keep this little place as backwards as it's always been. Stopping progress is like a sport to every one of you!"

A small crowd was gathering, and Dave Filson knew intuitively that it would be of little use to try to reply, so he folded his arms across his chest, gave the gathering crowd a slight smile, and listened as Amos Ray let him have it with two or three additional outrageous outbursts.

The principal had worked himself up into a serious frenzy, and Dave Filson was content to just stand there and smile. But Ray went too far when he asked, "Why don't you stick to tractors and farming and stuff you know about and quit butting into things you don't understand?"

In a flash, Shorty Cornett stepped between the Principal and Filson and said in a firm and even voice, "Leave him alone. You've said enough. We're going into the gym now."

Amos Ray was out of control. He shouted at Shorty, "Butt out, Hayseed. This has nothing to do with you!" And with that, he gave Shorty a jolting two-handed shove.

A lot happened in the next two seconds, and it happened in a blur. Someone shouted, "No, Shorty, no!" And at exactly the same second, Shorty Cornett delivered a dynamite left jab to the right side of Amos Ray's face and instantly followed with a thundering right hook that smashed into his left temple. Amos Ray reeled and keeled backwards, and someone caught him before he fell to the ground. Three or four men grabbed Shorty and hustled him back to the parking lot. The small-town talking started immediately.

* * *

The next morning, Jerry Brown was waiting alone in his office for the arrival of Amos Ray. He was sitting at his desk and recalling the comments of the board members at the emergency school board meeting the night before. They had heard of the events at the basketball game and were all livid with Principal Ray. Brown could still hear the words of Board Chairman Everett Juett when he had said, "Even the most ignorant fool in town would know not to push the likes of Shorty Cornett."

"Yes," Becca Switzer had said, "and this particular fool is trying to teach us."

Jerry Brown's reflections ended when the principal walked in. Amos Ray looked terrible: his face was swollen; he had a bandage over his left eye and an ugly abrasion on the right. He was not smiling when he spoke, "I've been thinking. What if I called everyone, including all teachers, and maybe a few parents into the auditorium and …."

Jerry Brown cut him off immediately, "No, Amos, it is over. It's over. Your tenure here is over."

"But I ..., what, what are you saying?"

"Today will be your last day. Last night the board voted six to zero to terminate you. I'm sorry Amos, but it just hasn't been a good fit. I'm sorry."

Amos Ray's voice trailed off and was hardly more than a whisper when he spoke, "Terminate?"

"Yes, Amos, You've been fired."

* * *

When they heard the news in the stripping room, nobody spoke for a few moments. Then one of the men said, "Well, that's that!" They worked mostly in silence for the rest of the day.

A Long Walk

Old John Lewis and his son Leon sat on the front porch of John's home. The dated but elegant house sat on a knoll that overlooked the river bottoms of John's cattle farm. It was late afternoon, and they had just finished a small two-man job. The men, one elderly and the other middle-age, were enjoying a cold beer before Leon left to return to his home and his law practice in the city. The autumn air was warm and clear, there was a pleasant breeze laden with the sweet fragrance that accompanies the transition of the fields and woods from summer to winter, and the vista was magnificent. The men were in no hurry to end their relaxing conversation.

The eminence of the knoll provided a clear view of the half-mile-long gravel driveway, the creek, and the farmland. The driveway was an interesting feature of John's homestead because it allowed John and his wife Dorothy to see an approaching car or truck long before it got to their house, and since his was the only house on the drive, anyone seen on the driveway was either coming to visit them or had no business there at all. What the two men noticed on this day was not a car or truck but what looked like a person walking.

What is that, Dad? Is that a person down by the

end?" Leon queried.

"I can't tell. It's not a deer is it? It's moving pretty slow."

"No, it's a person, definitely a person. A small person."

"It's a girl, Son, a small girl," John half shouted. "Get the truck!"

The two men wasted no time. They jumped into the pickup and headed down the drive to the girl. John got out almost before his son had the truck completely stopped. He approached the girl and saw immediately that she was crying uncontrollably. Old John was afraid that his towering frame would further frighten the little girl, so he dropped to his knees, held out his hand, and touched the girl's arm in a comforting gesture. The men tried to question the girl, but she was crying so hard that they couldn't make out anything she was trying to say.

Finally, the little girl nodded her head when Leon asked, "Aren't you Lafayette Sears' girl?" She then mumbled a few words that both men interpreted to be something about a school or school bus.

* * *

Rock Creek Elementary school had been serving the little hamlet of Mt. Zion, Kentucky and the surrounding countryside for generations. There was nothing unusual about the building, the teachers, or the students. They all had their roots in the red clay hill country around Mt. Zion. The farms were small, the buildings modest, and the people hard working and mostly honest. There were six classrooms in the old school house, and they were separated by the long wide hallway typical of the structures of their age. The principal's office was in the center with a small cafeteria at one end.

Eleven year old Annie Sears had always had a penchant for daydreaming in school, but on this October day she was lost in a complete fog. Her fifth grade class was listening as their teacher Miss Julia Browning reviewed the important points for an upcoming exam, but Annie was deep in her own private thoughts. She wasn't hearing a word her teacher said.

"Are you with us Annie?" asked Miss Browning

loudly and rather forcibly.

Annie was startled. "Uh, oh, yes, Miss Browning," she answered.

"Well, please pay attention."

The young student tried to keep her mind on Miss Browning's teaching, but it was a useless effort. In a few moments she was again lost in her own thoughts. The teacher once more observed that Annie had drifted off, but this time she chose to just let it go and say nothing. Most everyone was aware of Annie's difficult circumstances at home, and certainly, Ms. Browning was no exception. Not knowing for sure what new and upsetting event the child could be facing led the teacher to a belief that it would be better just to leave Annie alone with her thoughts.

* * *

Annie's troubles began the day she was born. She was the only child of the unstable and notorious Lafayette "Faye" Sears. Sears was a serious alcoholic who drifted from job to job and house to house. When the citizens of Mays County needed a casual laborer, they would usually call on Faye Sears. He was a dependable hand in the hay and tobacco fields, and he could be counted on as long as he started the day sober. If Faye was on a drunk, which was certainly not a rare thing, he was basically incapacitated.

Lafayette Sears was born into one of the more prominent families of the community and was well provided for from infancy until early adulthood. Sears was one of the very few adolescents of Mays County able to attend the State University, but he was suspended and then kicked out after only one year. It was at the college that he was introduced to alcohol, lost his innocence, and gave up all commitment to responsibility.

The summer following Faye's year in college, he promptly got Yvonne Wells pregnant. Yvonne came from a poor and broken family of notorious slackers, and although she too was somewhat irresponsible, she was not nearly as unstable as Lafayette Sears. The two were married, mostly drank and fought, and stayed together until the child, Annie, was about a year old. It was then, and nobody around Mt. Zion really knew why, that Yvonne deserted Sears and the girl. She left the farm country, moved to somewhere near Cincinnati, and was rarely ever heard from after that.

From that moment, Lafayette Sears' life was punctuated by a series of unproductive and questionable changes. He moved with his young but growing daughter from one ramshackle tenant house to another. He was constantly getting rid of one worn out wreck of a car or pickup and trading for another of the same condition. He began to drink more heavily and in a short time became hopelessly addicted.

If there was one thing that was consistent in Faye Sears' broken life, it was his propensity for taking up with one disreputable woman after another. As soon as one would pack up and leave, Faye wasted no time in looking for another to move in with him and take her place. He was often heard saying that the women in his life were "hot and spicy", but the ladies around Mt. Zion were more apt to refer to them as "tramps."

For the most part, the women in Sears's life were good to Annie. She was a sweet, quiet, and mannerly child who rarely made any demands that could have led to friction around their home. Annie didn't say much, didn't have much, and didn't expect much.

When a new woman moved in, all of Faye Sears' attention would be showered upon her. Annie would be mostly left to make do for herself. But when one moved out, Sears gave more of himself to his daughter. He would stay sober for longer periods, cook and clean around the place, and engage Annie in conversation and long walks. This pleasantly stable period never lasted long: in a short time, Sears would show up with another rough looking floozy on his arm, the both of them all smiling and bubbling over. The pattern was fixed.

It was sometime early in the fall of that year that Faye brought in a woman who was somewhat different than the standard. Paula Arnold was much younger and, without doubt, more beautiful. She dressed nicely and didn't seem to be as worn out and seedy as his usual live-ins. She didn't say much, mostly just slept late, got up, and then spent the day sitting around. She wasn't particularly nice to Annie.

This time Faye Sears went completely crazy. He couldn't get enough of his new lady. Sears was never far from her. He hardly went to work and mostly just hung around his latest dilapidated house trying to get Paula alone in the house, in the pickup, in the woods behind the house, or anywhere else that was handy.

It wasn't long before Paula had had enough. She packed up and left for her sister's home in Indianapolis saying she had to rest up and, "Get herself back together." That night Lafayette Sears drank himself silly, crying and slobbering.

* * *

It was the next day at the Rock Creek Elementary School that Annie Sears was having such a difficult time keeping her mind on her teachers' words. She was absorbed in her own personal thoughts. Annie could hardly wait for the school day to be over when she would get on the school bus and take the short ride home.

She was certainly aware of the departure of Paula Arnold, and to Annie, that meant a little attention from her father. All day she was wrapped up in her excitement. These were her favorite times. In her mind, Annie had the whole afternoon and evening mapped out. She was sure that history would repeat itself, and she was confident that she knew what the next few days would be like. There would be some pleasant times for her. She always yearned for her father's love and attention, and now some would be coming her way. Her father wouldn't be all wrapped up in Paula and would actually be happy to see her when she got home from school. They would talk, and they would probably sit down to the table and eat together. Things would be nice.

She was also hoping for an outfit to wear. On many of the previous occasions when Faye's women deserted him, he bought his daughter a brand new dress. She was hoping and praying that when she got home her father would have a package for her and in the package would be something from Newman's Department Store in town. Most of Annie's clothes and shoes were used hand-me-downs and came from thoughtful ladies, the church, or other charitable organizations in the community. A brand new dress was the best possible treat. Annie Sears daydreamed all morning, and as the afternoon wore on, her excitement mounted. When the bell rang ending the school day, she bounded out of the classroom and down the hall. She flew out of the building and down the terrace to the waiting school bus.

* * *

The bus ride to Annie's home took only about 10 minutes. Faye Sears's latest abode was a small tenant house just off the old highway. The old road was still maintained when the new highway was built because it continued to service two houses. The Sears' dwelling was one of them, and John Lewis's farm was the other. Right before the road ended in a dead end, Faye's rock driveway veered off and trailed straight up a steep bank to the small, old, frame structure. The instant the school bus stopped, Annie Sears bolted out the door, crossed the road, and scampered up the rough and steep driveway.

The first thing that Annie noticed when she reached the top of the hill was the empty parking place under the huge locust trees. Faye Sears was not at home. Then she was surprised to see the front door had been left standing wide open. When she walked into the home it was obvious that not only was Faye Sears not in most of their belongings were gone as well.

Annie Sears was staggered. She ran back outside and began to call for her father. She screamed and called as she ran through the deserted hog lot, past the chicken coops, and to the old barn looking for her father, but he didn't answer, and she couldn't find him. Annie was overcome with fear: she had begun to think that someone had kidnapped or killed her father, stolen all of their belongings, and driven off in her father's truck. Annie crumbled to the ground and burst out crying. She was unable to move, and she couldn't control her crying.

When finally she was able to get up, she realized that she had to get help for her father and for herself as well. Of course, Faye Sears didn't have a telephone, so Annie began the walk that would take her to the nearest neighbor. She went down the driveway and followed the deserted highway to the lane at John Lewis's farm. She was hesitant to enter, but after a few moments, Annie started up the long driveway towards his house. She was overcome with fear, confusion, and anxiety. The young girl was crying so hard and shaking so violently that she could hardly walk. After she had staggered and walked about a hundred yards, she saw the pickup truck coming down the drive towards her.

* * *

The big living room at the center of John Lewis's home was spacious with high ceilings and more than ample room. John had started a small fire in the huge stone fireplace to knock out the slight chill that early autumn had brought to his house. John's wife, Dorothy, had walked to the garden with Annie Sears, and that left John, Leon, and Sheriff Rocky Stone in the room to hash out what exactly had happened, and what should be done.

Earlier, when John and Leon had Annie safely in the hands of Dorothy, they had driven to Lafayette Sears's home and found it abandoned exactly as the little girl had described. It was then that John called his long-time friend Sheriff Stone and suggested to him to come out as quickly as he could. Rocky wasted no time. As soon as the sheriff heard the details and digested the seriousness of the happenings, he radioed his deputy and instructed him to, "Find Faye Sears and find him right now!"

While they were waiting to hear from the deputy, Sheriff Stone called Bonnie Franklin, the social services representative, and informed her of what had happened. She said she would be right out. His cell phone began ringing as soon as he ended that call.

The sheriff answered the incoming call, advised the other men that it was his deputy, and walked out to the front porch to talk. When he re-entered the room, Rocky was obviously agitated, and as was his nature when stressed, he spoke in a crisp and rather loud way. "Well, the sonofabitch has really done it this time. He is gone. He pulled into Riggs's service station to gas up about noon. His pickup was loaded down with all the junk he owned. When Riggs asked him where he was headed, Sears told him he was going to Indianapolis to find that last chick he was living with. Evidently she had packed up and left him. He was blubbering and said he couldn't live without her. Riggs said it was obvious that Faye was half drunk. Riggs tried to talk him out of driving. Sears just grunted, waved him off, and left."

"Well shit fire, now what?" John questioned.

"I'm going in and see if maybe, by some miracle, he's still around town somewhere. Maybe he stopped at the pool hall. And I'll see where that social worker is," the sheriff said while moving toward the door. "She should be here."

Sheriff Stone touched his hat in a signal of departure and then added, "If you can, stay put. I'll be right back, or I'll call."

There was a long moment's silence before John turned to his son and questioned, "Now what Leon, What's next?"

Leon was silent for a few seconds and then he answered his father. "Well Dad ... let's see now. If Faye left and deserted his daughter, and it looks like that is exactly what has happened, it will probably unfold like this. There will be a criminal charge of parental neglect and abandonment. Once made, the charges will be prosecuted by the County Attorney. If Sears has left the state, he will be extradited back to our county. The end result will be that he will be stripped of custody of the girl, he will be jailed, and Annie will become a ward of the state."

"So what will they do with her?"

"The state will attempt to find family kin to assume custody," Leon answered.

"I don't think Faye has any relatives."

"Then they will try to find suitable adoptive parents. Sometimes a friend will petition the court for guardianship. However it goes, it's not going to be pleasant."

John and Leon finished the conversation as they were walking out of the big room and onto the porch. They once again sat down to wait for the arrival or call from Sheriff Stone. They sat mostly in silence as they pondered the afternoon's happenings.

They watched as Dorothy Barnes and Annie walked around in the garden. Each was carrying a basket. "It looks like the girl's quit crying, Dad," Leon half whispered. "She's walking a little bit better."

John didn't reply, but dropped his head. His shoulders slumped.

Leon was startled by his father's silence and posture.

"What's wrong Dad?" the son asked. "Are you all right?"

John raised his head, straightened his shoulders, and spoke quietly, "Just thinking son, just thinking."

Old John Lewis slowly stood up, paused for just a second, turned to Leon and then added, "Somebody's gotta tell the little girl. Somebody will have to tell her."

The Courage of Peachy Cornett

The mid morning was cool, crisp, and pleasant for Adam "Peachy" Cornett. It was early spring, and he was walking into the big woods that he had purchased two years earlier. For Peachy, the huge wooded tract was a fine addition to his small tobacco and cattle farm. He first began hunting, fishing, and foraging in and around the big woods before he had reached his teenage years and during the last thirty years hardly a day passed without his having entered the place. As he angled down the hillside path that led to the deepest part of the big woods, he smiled to himself with gratitude: he was thankful for his good fortune to have been able to own this unique piece of property.

The wooded acreage had two distinguishing features that set it apart from the typical farmstead around the little community of Mount Zion, Kentucky. The place consisted of 250 acres, and that made it much larger than the usual farm, and more importantly, the land consisted mostly of old growth timber. The huge woodland was believed to be one of only five virgin timber stands remaining in the state, and Peachy believed that it was providential that he had title to such magnificent land.

For almost half a century, the wooded farm belonged to an absentee owner named Wilson Wright. Hardly anyone around Mt. Zion had ever seen him or even remembered him having bought it. When Wright died, the farm, known appropriately as the "old Wright place", was sold to another set of absentee owners. These new owners lived and worked in Cincinnati, and their only intent was to use the land for hunting. They posted the farm the day after they bought it and immediately tacked up no-trespassing signs around the entire perimeter. Casual use of the land by the populace around Mt Zion came to a halt. There was no more hunting or fishing excursions into the woods. The popular nature walks of young lovers and even the annual Rock Creek Elementary School science projects were forbidden. When the new absentee owners were forced to sell the place because of the severe economic downturn, Peachy Cornett jumped at the chance to buy it. He mortgaged his existing farm, withdrew his savings, and became the new owner at the Master Commissioner's sale.

On this day, Peachy was walking into the woodland to check on two turtle lines he had set in the creek that ran through the farm. Rock Creek had its beginning on the sloping forested hillsides, and the springs that emanated along its banks gave it a pristine and pure beginning. As Peachy slipped quietly into the woods, he became one with the forested element. His huge six foot and five inch frame belied his graceful and gentle nature. He was generally a quiet man, and he became almost soundless when he was in this setting.

Peachy angled off to the north and headed down the sloping hillside towards the first and largest of two deep water holes that were on his property. Both of the large pools were buried deep in the old growth section of his property. The big forest was home to the uncut and ancient old-growth timbers.

Peachy Cornett had traversed the hillside and was deep into the big forest when he stopped at a small patch of chanterelle mushrooms. Their bright orange color got his attention from about thirty feet away. For Peachy, the sight of these wavy looking mushrooms was always a cause for enthusiasm: the chanterelle had a nice flavor when sautéed. He made a mental note of where they were growing and decided to take a slight detour on his way to the creek and look for some morels too. The morels came up every year in the deep shaded forest and were considered the tastiest of all mushrooms.

Just as Peachy stepped away from the mush-rooms, he heard the warning cry of the ever vigi-lant crow. The alarm was coming from much deep-er in the woods, and in a few moments, a second and then a third crow joined the first in the pierc-ing alarm-cry. From the sound and the intensity of the racket, Peachy knew at once that the crows had spotted either a chicken hawk or a human. He reasoned that since it was the middle of a weekday afternoon and nobody had asked him about visit-ing his woods the cause for the crow's alarm was surely the hawk.

Before Peachy had moved but a few steps, he heard the rustle of what he knew were deer run-ning, jumping, and moving through the woods, and he also reckoned correctly that they were moving straight towards him. It was only seconds before three yearlings and two older does passed closely by. They had been bedded down, were startled, and ran from the direction of the sentry crows. Cornett knew then that a person or people were on his property. Deer would pay no attention to a chicken hawk.

* * *

Mt. Zion, Kentucky was a tight, close-made, little place. The hamlet was a remote crossroads community comprised of 10 to12 small houses along the highway that ran straight through the small town. In addition, there were a couple of churches, the cemetery, McBride's store, Riggs' service station, and a few more homes situated on a couple of side streets.

The area around Mt. Zion was red-clay hill country. The farms were mostly small and the land poor. There were nice, flat, and productive ridge lands that gave way to hollows on each side. The sloping hillsides were used for pasture and hay fields; usually the steepest were wooded. Sometimes there were narrow bottoms along the creeks and branches at the foot of a hill.

The farmers of Mt. Zion raised tobacco, and they had since the place was first settled. The nature of the land combined with the humid weather provided the perfect conditions for growing the crop. There was just enough rich land along the narrow ridges and creek bottoms on almost every farm to plant, nurture, and harvest an acre or two of burley tobacco. The crop provided the cash supplement that allowed the farmers and their families to remain and live on the small farms. Raising a tobacco crop was labor-intensive, and neighbors helping neighbors during setting time and harvesting time was crucial to the success of everyone. Sharing equipment and tools was equally important.

The exchange of labor and equipment led naturally to a social intimacy. The people of Mt. Zion shared their lives with those who lived around them: there were very few secrets.

News traveled fast around Mt. Zion. The daily gatherings at the card table in McBride's store, the meetings before and after church, and the telephone calls among the lady folk all served as conduits for the exchange of news and opinions about the events, the status of the crops, who was doing what, and all else perceived as important.

Peachy Cornett began to ask around if anyone had seen something or knew anything about who might have been on his land. He was convinced of his interpretation about the deer and the crow. It was universally understood that friends, neighbors, and the populace around Mt. Zion were welcome to visit the woods, but it was also understood that courtesy required that Peachy be informed either before or immediately after the visits. Strangers were considered trespassers, and the farmers all looked out for the property of their neighbors. Hardly any infringement or trespass went unnoticed.

Jake Barnes and Ernie Stone lived and farmed

across the road from each other, and their properties both joined the land of Peachy Cornett. It was not unusual for them to meet at the gate of one or the other in the course of their work. They both enjoyed the short conversations that ensued and the chance to catch up on a little news.

"Have you seen Peachy?" Asked Jake Barnes when their paths crossed early one morning.

"Saw him yesterday. I think he's raking hay back on his creek-side ridge."

"I need to borrow his big wagon. I'll get over there later and find him." said Jake.

Ernie nodded and then questioned, "Did he ask you if you'd seen anyone around his place?"

"Yeah, he's been asking around. You know how he is. He said something about crows and some deer."

"He's sure someone was in his big woods, and we all know how nervous he gets about that. I'd guess he's asked everyone he's seen." Ernie suggested.

Jake looked down, kicked around a little in the gravel, then looked up and said, "We all love to tease and laugh with Peachy, but when it comes to this kind of stuff, he's usually right."

"Young bird ought to be. He's spent enough time at it."

"You know," Jake added, "we all look out for Peachy. He's always been everybody's favorite, but if the truth be told, he's probably better able to take care of himself than most of us."

"Ain't that the truth?" Ernie said with a big grin as he nodded, gave his usual salute of departure, and finished with, "I'd better get to work."

* * *

Over the course of the next few days, Peachy Cornett occupied himself and his thoughts with raking and baling his hay fields. He put the matter of the perceived trespasser behind him, and when he was finished with the hay crop and again entered his big woods, he didn't give it a thought. Peachy was preoccupied with once more setting a few turtle lines, having a little time to fish the riffles for the big carp that were beginning to run, and then gathering up some mushrooms. As he eased quietly down the hillside towards the creek, he entered the biggest timber and oldest area of the forest.

There was an ancient cold-water spring along the banks of Rock Creek. Peachy had been thirsty all morning from the dehydration he always endured for a day or two after working in the hayfields. He headed directly for the spring. The vein was nestled between two giant sycamore trees, and the water flowing from the limestone outcropping was pure and pristine. Years ago, somebody had rocked in a small basin that became a reservoir for the cool water. An old enameled blue and white speckled dipper hung from one of the trees, and when Peachy took it down to drink from it, he was startled to see that the dipper had a small amount of water in it. That settles it, thought Peachy. He realized at once that someone had used the dipper and not completely emptied it; he hadn't been there for over a month, and it hadn't rained for two weeks. Peachy decided right then that he would intensify his surveillance. He was unsettled.

Peachy Cornett knew enough about himself to realize that being more observant wasn't the answer; he hardly ever missed a thing when he was in the woods. He would just have to spend more time in the forest walking, listening, and watching until he caught whoever was trespassing.

Peachy limited his farm work to checking his cows. They had finished calving, but it was the practice of all the good farmers around Mount Zion to observe their cattle at least once a day. He took his A.T.V. to the pasture fields, looked over his herd, sped straight back, fed the barn cats, and headed directly to his big woods where he would spend the remainder of the morning and afternoon. Later in the summer and autumn, the forest itself would provide him with his lunch, but because it was a little early for foraging, Peachy Cornett put some crackers and cheese in his coat pocket for his lunch. He approached his search with a relentless determination.

When in his woods, the big man began to see more signs that someone was on his place. He noticed where a flat rock had been added to the crossover place at the first riffle on Rock Creek. Peachy had been content to make the long stride from one dry rock to the next or sometimes just step in the inch deep water between the rocks. The additional rock had been placed: its placement was deliberate, and it was, without doubt, the result of human endeavor. All Peachy Cornett could do was stop and stare at the extra stepping stone. For him, it was the equivalent of seeing where someone had been in your living room while you were out. Peachy was baffled and becoming a little angry.

He went to the big woods as often as he could. He slipped around and over his land, but he saw no one. On the third day of his intensified search, he was surprised to see where a few wild flowers he called Dutchmen's Britches had been picked. They were cleanly broken off at the stem about six inches from the top, and only a few had been taken. There were a few signs that someone had walked cautiously among or around the flowers, and it was obvious that they had been careful.

Peachy left the small patch of flowers and head-ed straight to where he knew buffalo clover had always grown before. There were a few places in the deepest parts of his woods where this delicate wildflower grew, and the big man was well aware that the plant was on several endangered species lists. He had become protective of the clover and was anxious to see if anyone had disturbed the fragile perennial. When he approached the site, he was relieved to see that the clover was again growing and was undisturbed. As he surveyed the immediate area, he was again baffled. Peachy saw enough signs the deep humus to tell him for sure that somebody had, without doubt, been there. They had walked around the buffalo clover several times but never got closer than about five feet from the plants. This mystified Peachy Cornett.

* * *

Almost every day the farmers around Mt. Zion made the trip into the little community to stop by McBride's store, the radiator shop, or Riggs service station to catch up on what was happening, and certainly, Peachy Cornett was no exception. Everyone loved to see Peachy coming; he loved to tease and consequently was the subject and victim of never ending ribbing and jokes. His big frame and big laugh would fill a room. While he did somehow manage to graduate from high school, his abject lack of academic interests, coupled with the fact that at age 45 he had never married provided the catalyst for much of the fun.

"How's the big mystery going, Peachy? Have you caught that poacher yet?" asked Harold Browning when Peachy entered McBride's store after supper one evening

"It's probably one of you fools messing with me," was his reply.

Then old John Lewis jumped in with, "Peachy,

folks have been saying that you couldn't find them if the Chinese army marched through your place."

Peachy burst out laughing and replied with, "Sometimes folks is right, and sometimes folks is wrong, but when you-all is the folks, chances are its wrong." The men all laughed.

Everybody in that room knew how difficult it was to get onto Peachy Cornett's land without someone knowing. The big woods were bordered by Ernie Stone's land on one side and Peachy's own farm on the other. There was only about 100 feet of road frontage on the highway, and almost everybody traveled by there daily. If anyone parked on the small gravel pull-off place to walk into the forest, their car would be noticed. The people of Mt. Zion also knew that Peachy Cornett would allow anyone from the extended neighborhood to visit his land if they asked for permission.

There was a inborn sense within the community that the problems of one farmer became the problems of all, and certainly, the men were genuinely interested in what was going on with Peachy's farmland.

The mood in the big storeroom became more serious when John Lewis said, "Everybody's been watching Peachy. Nobody's seen a thing."

There was a murmur in the room as each of the seven or eight men present nodded and affirmed their shared concern.

* * *

His determination to find who was trespassing had become an obsession with Peachy Cornett. He was going into the big woods more frequently and was purposely going at all different times of the day. What he did not see was a human, but what he did see were more and more subtle signs that someone had been on the place. A cool early morning in June found Cornett again circling his old growth forest. As he approached the lower area of the hillside and was getting close to the creek, Peachy stopped abruptly, raised his head, and cupped his hand to his ear. He was hearing a low humming sound, but he couldn't identify exactly what it was, and that was unusual for him. As Peachy slipped down towards the creek, he again stopped to listen and try to identify the humming and its source. It was then that he knew. His heart began to race wildly, and he felt a staggering jolt of adrenalin. The noise was the high pitched humming of a person!

Peachy Cornett eased ever so carefully towards the sweet sounds, and when he was within twenty yards of the creek he saw its source. Sitting on the creek bank and facing across the creek, and away from Peachy was a woman or a young child. Cornett did not move but continued to watch. The musician was clearly eating and humming between bites. When she turned her head, Peachy got a clear look at who she was.

Oh my Gosh, Peachy thought to himself. It is Miss Patterson. Eva Patterson. How could I have forgotten? A year ago, maybe two, she asked me if she could visit the place. Of course I told her yes, any time. And how stupid of me. She could follow the old access road from her home through Ernie's place and follow the creek straight to here. And only climb or open one gate. How could I have not thought of her?

Peachy didn't move a muscle for the longest time. Then he slowly turned around and walked silently back up the hill to his house and farm. When he entered his home, he sat down at the kitchen table and began to digest the essence of what he had learned. He knew very little of Eva Patterson. He remembered when she moved to Mt. Zion three or four years earlier after her husband had died. She was some kind of scientist and worked at the State University in Lexington. Whenever he went to church, she was always there and sitting alone. She seemed to be pleasant, was slightly built and attractive. Peachy believed that she was in her late forties. If she was involved in the community in any way other than through church, Peachy was not aware of it.

The revelation that the lady had been spending so much time in his woods had him puzzled. Peachy lapsed into earnest thought. Why did she spend so much time on my land? How did she avoid being observed? Why was she so careful around the wildflowers? Did she come to the woods every day? What is all this with her? He now knew how she was entering his land, and he decided then that he would wait for her where the old road entered his place and confront her by "accidentally" running into her.

The next morning Peachy Cornett left his home and walked directly to a spot about forty yards above the place where he was sure the lady would be entering. He waited quietly, but she did not appear. He followed the same plan again on the next day, and he didn't wait long before he heard her approach. His heart was robustly beating when she first appeared. Cornett surprised himself when he remained absolutely motionless and did not approach the visiting Ms. Patterson. What he did do was remain above her on the hillside and shadow her as she walked up the creek-bank towards the old-growth section of his forested land.

The next two weeks found Peachy Cornett in his woods waiting for the enigmatic Ms. Eva Patterson to show up on his land. When she did visit the place, he always remained hidden from her and only watched the lady from afar. She carried a notebook, and moved very slowly through the woods. As she walked through his land, she would occasionally stoop down to examine a plant or peer for long periods into the tops of the trees. It seemed that nothing was escaping her inspection. Peachy was mystified by what she was doing, but he was equally confused by his own behavior. He could not explain to himself why he didn't just confront the lady and ask her to explain what she was doing. Again and again, he would find himself dwelling on his own thoughts. Why am I wasting my time following her? I just watch her. What am I doing? Why don't I confront her? People don't scare me, so that can't be it.

As the days passed, Peachy noticed that Eva Patterson would make some observations and notes as she walked through his land, but both activities became more intense when she reached the old growth section of the farm. He pondered why the lady would always make it a point to visit one area of the old farm first then go to a second more forested parcel before ending up in the old-growth section.

The entire 250 acres could be clearly divided into three distinct tracts. The ten-acre field along the highway was the last on the big farm to have been tended. Ernie Stone and Peachy himself had square-baled it seven or eight years earlier. The terrain sloped off to the left and towards the headwaters of Rock Creek. Small cedar trees were abundant on the little piece, and except for a few redbuds, the cedars were the only trees visible. Since no cattle had been in to the field to nip the foliage, the brush, weeds, and briars between the trees made walking difficult.

An old road dipped down and away from the cedar field, crossed the trickling creek, and entered a forest of much larger trees. This center portion of the old farm was abandoned perhaps a century before the small cedar and weed field by the highway. Scattered sparsely throughout this huge central part of the place were the huge sprawling seed-oaks that were there when the pasture was abandoned. They were ancient. Some were dead and some were dying. Surrounding them were the tall straight white oak, hickory, and ash trees that were in prime health and growing. These straight trees had competed for sunlight and grown forty or so feet straight up to where they formed a gentle canopy that mostly shaded the forest floor. Enough sunlight filtered through to provide an occasional splotch on the leaf covered ground. The cedars that once covered these fields couldn't survive the competition for sunlight, and only a few survived. They were mostly fully grown, but slowly dying for lack of sun. Random and rotting cedar skeletons could be seen lying about. The walking here was not as mean as in the small field by the road. The ground was a thick mat of dead leaves, hickory casings, and decaying acorns, small limbs, and sticks.

Following the creek upstream would lead to the deepest part of the forest. Here the trees were majestic, and the ancient woods spectacular. The trees were two and three feet in diameter and grew seventy-five to a hundred feet straight up. Each had just one trunk with no side branches until almost the very top where the branches reached out and formed a dense canopy. Little sunlight penetrated, and the forest was in a permanent semi-darkness.

Cedar trees were long gone, and only the hard-woods remained. The forest floor was thick with humus and clear of all weeds and undergrowth. The air was void of dust and pollen and within it hung a sweetness and a tranquility. The forest exuded a perpetual serenity.

Two weeks was enough. Peachy began to feel somewhat confused about his behavior. He was beginning to feel stupid wasting so much time. He decided that on his next rendezvous with the thirty-yard space between himself and Eva Patterson he would reduce the space to zero and position himself in a place where she would run directly into him. Peachy had no idea what would transpire at that point, but for him, something had to change.

Neighboring

* * *

There were six men at McBride's store that evening. Four were playing a game of euchre at the card table, and Peachy Cornett and BeeJay Browning were waiting to play the winners. When Eva Patterson walked through the front door, a hush fell over the room. It was unusual for women to visit McBride's at that time of the evening and, Ms. Patterson was practically a complete stranger to the men. All of the men except Peachy Cornett looked up and watched Eva. After his first glance, Peachy dropped his eyes to the card table.

When she had walked half-way across the big store room, Eva stopped and turned to the men. She looked sprightly, and her face was radiant: it was a blustery night and Eva's hair had blown down in wisps over her forehead. With her lower lip, she blew her hair up and out of her face, winked, and said to the men, "It's all right. I don't bite. You can go back to talking. I just came in to get some sugar."

BeeJay Browning mumbled something under his breath about "getting some sugar" that only Peachy Cornett could hear. Peachy slowly raised his head up and stared directly into BeeJay's eyes. At the same time, he ever so slightly raised up as if to come out of his chair, but he quickly settled right back down and again stared at the table. The move went unnoticed.

"Uh, Oh, hello, Ms. Patterson, how are you tonight? We didn't mean to stare. It's nice to see you," said John Lewis.

"Yes, and how have you been?" added old Jake Barnes sincerely.

With that brief exchange, the men resumed their card game, and Eva Patterson picked up the sugar. She paid McBride and turned around to walk out. When she was again beside the card table, she turned to the men and she asked, "Is this a men's only club, or can a woman join in the game?"

"Its euchre Ms. Patterson," said Ernie Stone. "Do you know how to play euchre?"

"Why, yes, I do," she replied.

"Well of course, we'd like to have you join the game," said Jake Barnes. "This round just ended. Peachy and BeeJay are both waiting to play the winners, and I'm sure one of them would agree to sit out another game so that you can play."

At that, BeeJay and Peachy turned to face each other. Peachy Cornett cleared his throat, stammered a little, and then said, "That's all right. You go ahead BeeJay, I really should be going now anyway." Peachy raised himself slowly out of the chair, said goodbye to those sitting around, nodded to Eva Patterson, shouted goodbye to Mr. McBride, donned his hat, and turned to walk out.

It was then, as Eva was moving towards the chair to sit down that she turned and said to Peachy, "Oh, Mr. Cornett, I do thank you so much for giving me permission to go onto your property."

Peachy had pivoted back around and was looking directly at the lady. He hesitated for just a moment before saying, "Any time, Ms. Patterson, any time." And with that, he walked out.

"Whose deal?" asked BeeJay as Eva Patterson sat down smiling to join the men and the game.

* * *

The next morning, Peachy was in the woods early, and Eva Patterson did run smack into him. He had placed himself next to a giant white-oak and had anticipated correctly and exactly where she would walk. Eva was within about five feet of the big man before she saw him. The lady made a slight startled jerk before calmly saying, "Why hello, Mr. Cornett, you startled me."

"Hello, Miss Patterson, I'm sorry; I should have whistled or made some racket when I heard you coming."

Eva Patterson didn't waste a second before explaining her presence on the farm. "I have been visiting your place here for several weeks now. I've been mostly interested in varieties of plant life that are rare or endangered, particularly in the old-growth part of your farm. Also, Mr. Cornett, I'm now sure that the old-growth part is, in fact, uncut virgin forest. I spent a lot of time studying that."

Peachy responded with, "Yes, Ms. Patterson, I am aware of your visits. And please call me Adam or Peachy."

Eva Patterson seemed surprised that Peachy was aware of her trips onto his land and looked at him inquisitively, but she said nothing about it. She changed the subject with her question to him, "Are you aware, Sir, that the Emerald Ash Borer is present in some of you trees?"

Peachy smiled to himself. He was amused that this lady, who seemed to be a few years older than he, would refer to him as "Sir". "Yes, ma'am," he said. "I do know about the beetle, but I haven't seen any signs or any damage. I didn't think they were in my woods, but I have been expecting the worst."

Eva Patterson responded with, "Well, they are there, and with your permission, I'm going there now. Would you have time to walk with me and let me show you how to tell of their presence?"

The two walked almost in silence as they traversed the hillside and entered into the old-growth forest. When in the deep refuge, Eva Patterson walked without hesitation to a large ash tree, put on her reading glasses, and ran her hands over the symmetrical and deep veined bark. "Here, Mr. Cornett." She exclaimed. "Look right here."

Peachy bent slightly to get a good look at the

small "D" shaped hole where the Ash Borer had entered. "So that's where he entered, huh"?

"Yes, Sir. And this tree is doomed." She answered.

Fortunately, there were only a few ash trees among the giants, but the big saw logs they would produce certainly had a significant value. Since they were going to die anyway, Peachy immediately began to mull over the possibility of cutting and harvesting the big trees. The only other option was to just to let them die, fall, and rot. "Is there any way to save them?" he asked.

"No, Mr. Cornett, they are going to die."

The big woodsman seemed to withdraw into himself, looked off, and walked in a rather large circle around the old tree. There was an ancient rust colored rotting tree trunk about twenty yards from the big ash. It was nothing more than an elongated mounded heap of humus almost like thick wet sawdust, and various small plants were beginning to grow from it. "How long would you say this old dead trunk has been laying here Ms. Patterson?" he asked.

"Maybe seventy-five to a hundred years." she replied.

He walked around and mused for a few more moments and then said, "I guess I'll just let them die and allow Mother Nature to take over. And please call me Peachy."

Eva Patterson smiled, nodded, and said, "OK, Peachy, and what about you and I splitting this chicken salad sandwich and the chips I brought for my lunch?"

"Uh...Well...OK," said Peachy, "but let's walk down to the spring to eat." He was thinking about the sack of crackers and cheese in his pocket and the cool watercress growing at the spring.

On the way to the deep spring, the two followed the game trail and ancient buffalo trace down the hillside. When they came upon a patch of the rare buffalo clover, they both stopped. "Is this what you're studying?" asked Peachy.

"Yes, buffalo clover and other uncommon plant-life."

"Its whole name is actually Running Buffalo Clover," said Peachy, and he emphasized the word, "running".

"Yes," Eva Patterson agreed, "and if we were to be

completely exacting, we could also call it *trifolium stoloniferum* of the family *fabaceae*."

Peachy Cornett knew just enough to realize that there were some kinds of scientific names for things, but he had no idea of why. He hesitated a moment and then exclaimed, "Well it seems to me that one name should be enough, and as far as what family it belongs to, I'll just say that since it's on my farm, it belongs to the Peachy Cornett family!" And with that, he burst out laughing and gently nudged Ms. Patterson with his elbow.

"Oh, you!" said Eva laughing.

As they continued down towards the creek, Cornett asked the lady frankly why she was spending so much time observing and studying on his property.

"Mr. Peachy," she replied, "I am a research biologist employed by the University. On campus I'm known as Doctor Patterson. My job is currently funded by a grant that we were able to get. The aim is to categorize and catalogue all plant life in the old-growth forests in Kentucky. The long-term goal is to preserve and stabilize the forests and their endangered species. It was just luck that I heard of this place of yours after I moved so close by. We knew of the four other old-growth forests in the state, but no one really knew about yours. Everyone involved in the study was excited when I was able to determine that your woods had never been cut. And please know that I am so grateful for your having given me permission to visit your property."

Peachy responded with, "Could've saved yourself a lot of time by just asking. I've always known the place was uncut."

Eva Patterson smiled to herself as they walked the remaining few yards to the spring.

When they reached the spring, Peachy stepped down below the water basin and grabbed a large handful of watercress from the cold running water. He carefully pulled the roots off, threw them aside, and then rinsed the small viney plants. Eva Patterson was sitting on the rock ledge above the creek and had her sandwich and chips spread out on a napkin when he climbed back up. The big man sat down next to her, took his cheese and crackers out, and put them on the napkin with her lunch.

"May I have some chips?" Peachy asked.

"Certainly," she replied, "help yourself."

Peachy then laid out the sack that his lunch had been in, took a few of the chips, crunched them up on the sack, and mixed them with the watercress. "Here, try this." he said as he offered the mixture to Eva.

"Oh-my-gosh that is tasty!" was her reply, and they both polished off the delicate appetizer before they shared and ate the rest of their food.

It was then that Eva complained of having a piece of the meal stuck between her teeth and lamented that she didn't have a toothpick. Peachy responded by standing up, walking a few feet to one of the giant ancient cedar trees, and breaking off one of the multitude of small snags that always line their trunks. With his pocket knife, he split the inch long piece into a perfect hard and pointed implement. "Here," he said as he handed it to Eva, "and ten times better than any you can buy anywhere."

They agreed to meet the next day so that Peachy could show her other places on his property where the buffalo clover grew. Once again she was bewildered as to how the man knew where she had and had not been, but again she said nothing.

From that day on, and for the next several weeks, they were together in the woods almost every day. The two would traverse the hillsides, each soaking up what the other knew. The couple checked the creek for endangered muscle-clams, took soil samples deep in the woods, photographed hundreds of plants, measured trees, and laughed and talked and laughed some more.

* * *

The weather that fine August morning was spectacular. As the worshippers filed into the First Christian Church, it was noticed by all that an unusually large assembly would be in attendance. It was looking like the entire membership was going to be there. Henry Barnes and Leon Lewis were there from Lexington, and even Shorty Cornett showed up.

Jake Barnes smiled at Harold and BeeJay Browning as they walked up the yard to the church. "Dang, Harold, what's the occasion? Has everyone had a full week of sinning?"

Browning chuckled as they walked over to the sycamore tree where it was the usual practice for a small group of men to gather for a little conversation and a last minute smoke before the service began. The men were talking and laughing when Peachy Cornett left the parking lot, walked up the sidewalk, nodded to the men, and headed straight into the church.

"What's with Peachy?" asked Jake Barnes. "He's usually the first one over here and the last one into the church."

"Who knows, and did you see his getup? Looks like he finally bought a new suit. And this one fits him!"

"Yeah, and where's he been? I've not talked to him in almost a month, and I've only seen him in passing." added Jake. "You have to wonder what's going on."

"You're right. It's like he just dropped out. Is somebody sick?"

"John Lewis said he saw him going into the Hawkinsville library." Bee Jay added.

"No way. Peachy Cornett in a library. No way!" Jake about half shouted.

The men all chuckled and nodded before Harold Browning ended the meeting with his suggestion that, "We'd better go in now."

Other than the large crowd, the service was not unusual in any way. Reverend Miller delivered his standard too-long sermon. There were the prayers for world peace, good weather for the crops, and for the sick and the homebound. Two or three old-time favorite hymns were enthusiastically sung.

When the announcements were made and the

service was over, Reverend Miller surprised his congregation when he raised both arms into the air in his usual method of asking for quiet and absolute attention, and he delivered the following invitation, "I now invite those of you who can to remain in the sanctuary to witness and help celebrate the joining in Holy Matrimony of Adam "Peachy" Cornett and Ms. Eva Patterson."

There was absolute silence followed by a slight murmur, and then somebody in the back started a slow rhythmical clapping: Clap..Clap..Clap. They were joined by one, and then another, until the entire congregation stood up and erupted in a thunderous applause.

It was then that Peach Cornett stood up, eased out of the aisle where he always sat and walked up and across to where Eva Patterson was sitting in her usual seat. He bowed slightly, smiled and took her hand. The couple walked together to the front of the sanctuary where Reverend Miller was waiting. They were joined on their left by Peachy's brother and sister: Shorty Cornett and Dorothy Lewis. To the couples right stood Dorothy's husband, John Lewis, and their foster child, Annie Sears.

* * *

The next evening after supper, the usual gang of loafers was hanging out at McBride's store, and of course, the main topic was Peachy's wedding. Mostly the men expressed complete surprise. They were serious in their exclamations of dismay. Naturally, before long everyone got to laugh at BeeJay Browning when he told the small crowd that he knew it all along. For the most part, they seemed genuinely happy for Peachy.

In a few moments, Old Jake Barnes surprised everyone when he said these words, "My, my. What a sad occasion."

"Whoa Jake, how can you say that? What do you mean? Why are you calling it sad?"

"Well," Jake grinned and said, "Now we have one less thing to tease him about."

Watch for Mark Mattmiller's next work.

Check mark mattmiller on facebook

CPSIA information can be obtained at www.ICGtesting.com
Printed in the USA
LVOW06s0936190813

348448LV00004B/8/P